One Day With A Goat Herd

C. J. Stevens

John Wade, Publisher
Phillips, Maine

One Day With a Goat Herd
Copyright © 1992 by C. J. Stevens
All rights reserved, including the right to reproduce this book or
portions thereof in any form.
Published by John Wade, Publisher
P.O. Box 303, Phillips, Maine 04966

Library of Congress Cataloging in Publication Data
Library of Congress # 91-67945
ISBN # 0-9623934-7-9 cloth
ISBN # 0-9623934-6-0 paperback

First Edition
Printed in the United States of America

Acknowledgments

I wish to thank Diane Dishner for the time she gave me in sharing her experiences as a keeper of goats, for patiently answering my questions, and for giving me encouragement.

I also thank Amber and April Smith, and Alex Jamshidnejad for allowing me to photograph them with the herd.

I particularly appreciate the suggestions and corrections made by Elizabeth Bettencourt, Jane Considine, and Phoebe Erricson.

Further acknowledgments are made to Lyle Dishner, David Jamshidnejad, Nathan and Courteney Tulles, Roy and Sue Taylor.

Dedication

I dedicate this book to my goat friends: Cindra, Clover, Conrad, Czar, Fawn, Giselle, Gretchen, Hansel, Kiaya, Sonny, Speckles, Tania, Tatiana, Tracy, Tyrel, and Wish.

Introduction

This book is about a small herd of goats. There are sixteen of them: two bucks, seven does, and seven kids. They live on a small farm just outside the coastal town of Gold Beach in the state of Oregon. It is a mixed herd of seven Toggenburgs and nine Nubians. They are not exceptional individually or as a group—just good American grade and purebred stock. I could have selected Saanens, Alpines, Oberhasli, LaManchas, even scrub goats, and I might have if I had come across any of the others first.

Getting to know these particular Toggenburgs and Nubians was a matter of chance. My wife and I often spend several weeks during the winter months on the Oregon Coast for walks along the trails and beaches. One night while we were entertaining friends, the conversation shifted to goats. Like us, the couple had had them. The more we talked and shared experiences, the more I realized that I had enjoyed those days when we farmed in a limited way and kept a few goats.

"I wouldn't mind having them again," I remember saying, and realizing that our lives had changed and those days were gone for good, I added: "It would be fun writing about them."

"If you want to do that," said the woman, "I know of someone here in town who keeps them, and I'll gladly call her for you."

What drew me to these animals and what made them special to me on my first visit were the love and care the operator of this farm gave her entire menagerie of goats, sheep, lambs, rabbits, and bantams. Kindness and understanding not only create feelings of trust and a desire for bonding but give room for growth. I had seen too many cases in which neglect and unintentional cruelty to animals caused them to be rendered lifeless and shells of themselves.

Diane Dishner has had goats for nearly a decade, and she would be the first to admit that she has made her share of mistakes in raising them. But Diane's sensitivity to the herd, that awareness of belonging to it, has never wavered. She has many responsibilities to her goats, beyond the routine and unexpected decisions that must be made in their lives. She is a mother to the bucks, a queen to the does, a kid to the milkers, and a second mother to the kids. From these intricate bonds, Diane gets in return animals that are loving and faithful, and best of all she has the pleasure of being with them.

I visited the farm twice a week for more than two months, and during that time I took several hundred photographs from every conceivable position. I found myself leaning against wire fences, kneeling in the mud, and once lying flat on my stomach at the manure heap. Another inconvenience, though amusing when I look back on those visits, was my association with a bantam rooster called Black Bart. I would see him strutting and sidestepping in my direction, and he would be looking me straight in the eye. Then up he would fly on my shoulder, and with another flap of wings he would perch on my bald head and let loose his ungodly cry.

The herd was restive at first and not always the willing subjects I had hoped to find. It wasn't my presence that made them uneasy, but the whine of the camera lens bringing them into focus. Only Wish, a Toggenburg doe, found the courage to come forward and sniff at the fussy black box. I would take breaks after machine-gunning a roll of film and move among them in the pasture so we could get better acquainted. After the first half hour of every visit, we all settled down: they went back to their workaday world of browsing, chewing their cud, keeping their order of dominance, visiting the water trough and mineral lick; I, to loading another roll of film, darting around them, and standing motionless while hoping for a photograph that would say something special to me about them.

I had four gratifying interviews with Diane Dishner, and she went out of her way in sharing her experiences, lending me books on goat husbandry, and bringing in several young people so I could photograph them with the herd. It was my intention in the beginning to produce a book of photographs and text for very young readers, the five- to eight-year-olds, but somewhere early in the first draft my material took an unexpected turn and I found myself being swept elsewhere. I realized then I wanted to set aside one day in the lives of these animals for readers of most ages, and particularly for people who had never really met goats.

The weather turned warmer in late March along the Pacific as the coastal towns began preparing for their summer visitors. I knew it was time for us to leave for our home in Maine. We would miss our long walks on the trails and beaches and our new friends we had made at the farm. Sonny, the Nubian buck, was at the fence when we drove up to say goodbye. My wife pulled choice bits of clover that were beyond his reach, and we both stroked him. At the far edge of the pasture, the herd was browsing. I watched them for several long moments before turning away.

As a way of ending this introduction, I make my beginning here. Let me introduce the goats you are about to meet. First, there is Sonny, and sharing his enclosure is the buck called Czar, a Toggenburg. Beyond their fence, in another pasture, are the does and kids. The Nubian does are Cindra, Tatiana, and Kiaya; and the Toggenburg females are Wish, Tracy, Fawn, and Giselle. In deference to the herd it should be pointed out that Wish is the queen goat, the boss. Then there are all the scampering kids. Hansel and Gretchen are Toggenburgs; Conrad, Clover, Tyrel, Tania, and Speckles are the Nubians.

This is their book.

One Day With A Goat Herd

Sunrise

It is morning. Already the sun is mixing its pink, yellow and maroon splashes of color on the palette of the horizon, and a Douglas fir stands mysteriously at the top of a distant hill. The Pacific is calm now, an unbelievable turquoise, and the ocean swells from the northwest are too slight for whitecaps. Traffic on the coast road increases, and more lights are on than off in houses.

Up Euchre Creek Road, north of Gold Beach and next to a wood products mill, there are several small sheds joined together and ringed with fences. It is a place easy to miss in daylight, but at this hour of the morning it almost disappears into a blend of foliage and mist.

Inside one of these sheds, goats are stirring after a night of sleep. They stretch before standing, reluctant to move at first. The adult goats are all females in this part of the barn: doelings, pregnant does, and the new mothers.

The earliest to rise moves to a manger and sniffs the remnants of last night's hay. She is hungry, having twins to nurse, but her disdain for left-over food is greater than her appetite. She is drawn to the open doorway. Her eyes widen as she peeks around the opening and sees a curtain of mist parting above the water trough. She knows now that she is more thirsty than hungry, but the way the mist is prowling across the pasture and into the yard causes her to be suspicious. Should I chance it?—she seems to be asking. What should I do?

It is too early for Diane. They must wait to be milked, given their grain rations, and fed hay. The more wide awake ones gather at the doorway and slowly go out single file to the trough for water. One doe stops at the mineral box before joining the others by the gate. They are impatient already, and it is early. If their mistress is late, there will be a choir of bleating.

What are these creatures that man has kept for centuries and often maligns? Goats have been on this planet for five million years. They have roamed great distances from the early civilization centers, across Europe and Asia, into Africa, and have undergone the adaptive changes necessary to endure all kinds of climates.

It is believed that goats first appeared in southwest Asia near the end of the Pliocene age. They evolved from a rocky region that had limited vegetation. Because of scant feeding grounds, these animals established an intricate herd society of small bands capable of foraging in vast territories. They were graced with surefooted-ness, courage, and intelligence—three necessary traits for surviving under such difficult conditions.

Then in stepped man. The pastoral nomads of nearly ten thousand years ago not only coaxed the wild dogs to their camp-fires, but by supplying forage and through bonding they also tamed the goats and got in return a dependable source of meat, milk, cheeses, and skins.

The lives of the goats were made easier by domestication, but it did little to change the social structure of the herd. Goats went on being goats from central Asia to the Nile. It was man who was altered by this taming, and he found the new options irresistible. Gone was the necessity of drifting about in search of food. With skins to make containers and clothing, with goat hairs that could be woven into tents, the roaming tribes soon established permanent settlements.

But the practice of making use of the goat wasn't limited to the new villages. Wherever there was movement in the world, the goat accompanied man or soon followed. As a source of fresh milk, many sea explorers, including Columbus and England's Captain Cook, had several milking goats aboard ship when sailing for dis-tant lands.

Some Alpine goats had an unusual adventure with Napoleon. His soldiers had to carry much of their food with them when they went into battle. It was while troops were passing through Switzerland that food supplies changed. One night, when it was dark and the farmers were asleep, some of Napoleon's men crept into pastures and stole the goats. They milked the animals, and after breakfast when it was time to move out, they took the goats with them. Napoleon, or perhaps one of his able officers, had decided that it was easier to milk these four-footers that marched beside them than to carry extra provisions.

Sea captains returning from the British colonies in Africa and Asia during the late eighteen hundreds were quick to adopt the practices of Napoleon and the early navigators. They knew that the best possible shipmate for a passenger wasn't a talkative colonial but a good-natured milking goat safely housed below deck. And when the voyage was over the lucrative transactions would begin. Goat breeders and livestock auctioneers would hurry to the docks to purchase these animals for waiting clients.

Tatiana

She is drawn to the open doorway. Her eyes widen as she
peeks around the opening and sees a curtain of mist parting
above the water trough.

8:00 a.m.

Time for Diane. 8:00 a.m. The herd has been waiting for the sound of a vehicle in the drive. Wish, Tracy, and Fawn stand by the gate. The others are back in the barn. The mist has taken its ghostly presence elsewhere, and the sunlight is brighter and warmer. If Diane is late, both Wish and Fawn will find a place to sun themselves. But Tracy has another reason for being outside. Her twins, Hansel and Gretchen, are now in another shed at night, and from the gate she can hear them better when they answer her calls.

Separating the kids from Tracy is the beginning of time spent apart with only their peers for company. The kids learn greater independence, and the Dishners have more milk for their own use. The twins are bigger now and better able to take care of themselves. After the second week on the Dishner farm, the youngsters have different quarters at night. Within a few days, Tatiana's Tyrel and Tania, and Cindra's Conrad and Clover will experience the first pangs of being away from their mothers temporarily.

A vehicle approaches and pulls into the drive. The sound of a door slamming and footsteps in the early morning is a highlight of any day. They know who has arrived, and the uproar comes from every direction: does, bucks, kids, sheep, a ram, lambs, roosters, hens—all voicing demands. Only the rabbits are patient after the long night and take no part in this bedlam.

Their mistress hurries from one shed to another as the chores get underway. She has done them so many times that her motions are automatic. She knows most of the shortcuts and what this mixed lot of noisy residents expect from her. The feed is measured and fed—not too little and not too much. Diane also keeps an anxious eye on animals that may scour or have any of the other dozens of ills.

There is only one daily milking in springtime when the does freshen on the Dishner farm. Some goat keepers insist on two trips to the milk stand, but Diane has no intention of adopting a new routine unless it will benefit the herd. She is well aware that husbandry practices vary among handlers and differences are heatedly disputed. After milking, the kids are back with their dams for the day. This way there is an adequate milk supply for the Dishners and any orphan kids and lambs. Such a routine encourages the hungry kids to start nibbling alfalfa hay and grain.

The does are given their grain while they are being milked. They love these rations and willingly let down their milk. Diane is at this time bonded to them as a kid. The warm wash water to clean their udders, the feel of the milker's hands on them, and the pleasures these goats get in consuming the rich grain are things looked forward to and remembered. The rattle of a goat's neck chain, the licking and chewing, and the splash of milk in a pail are comforting sounds. The others wait their turns beyond the partition.

The hayracks are filled after the does have been milked. There is no ballroom decorum here. The only semblance of politeness is shown to Wish, the queen goat. She chooses her place to feed and the others follow. They pull at the hay, scattering half of it in their haste to get their share.

Tracy has her grain while being milked

Diane Dishner

8:45 a.m.

The morning chores have been done. 8:45 a.m. Diane leaves the milk room and crosses the drive to check on Sonny and Czar, the two bucks sharing a smaller pasture away from the does and kids. Since Sonny is the dominant male, having none of Czar's shyness, he is the one that rushes to the fence when his mistress appears.

Sonny is a bottle-raised American Nubian with the name of Talgerlin Sonny Beige. Red with white spots, he was born in Roseburg, Oregon and came from the Talgerlin herd. Diane thought Sonny Beige was an odd name for a bright red buck until she saw his papers—the sire's name was Oak Gold Ladykiller! Sonny was purchased when he was a few days old and the new owner lovingly spoiled him. Diane got Sonny when he was nineteen months old, and immediately she could see there was going to be a discipline problem.

Rebellious by nature, Sonny soon established himself as a "pushy" character. When he thought he wasn't being watched, he turned on his pasture mate, then a ram sheep, and tried to start a fight. His favorite tactic was to attack the ram's hindquarters by shoving and butting.

Unfortunately, the bullying didn't stop with the ram. Sonny began to question Diane's authority when she told him how to behave. When Czar was turned out to pasture with him, Sonny constantly made life miserable for the poor Toggenburg. Not just little shoves to establish dominance, but hard, swift butts. Soon, Sonny no longer cared if he was seen abusing others.

Diane realized that something radical had to be done. She wasn't going to have Sonny Beige out of control. Such a situation would be unbearable for her and not good for the herd.

It took both Lyle and Diane Dishner to grab Sonny, get him to the ground, and hog-tie him with a rope. They left him lying there for ten minutes and watched him closely. They could see that it was a shameful experience for such a proud buck, though it did have satisfying results. Sonny realized that he wasn't going to boss Diane and he had better change his ways. Once the rope was untied, he immediately showed signs of having been humbled, and with the loss of some of his immense pride he has been a better behaved goat.

Sonny's bullying tactics and bad behavior weren't entirely character flaws. They are survival traits found in most proud and active males. His one mistake was thinking that this handler could be dominated.

In the wild, a king buck's reign is peaceful as long as he rules with authority and is obeyed. He must act swiftly when he is challenged by one of the more courageous younger males. A king doesn't allow a challenge to go unnoticed, and the upstart can expect a sound thrashing. It's no longer a butt or shove or two as practiced on Czar and the ram sheep, but a fight that won't be forgotten.

If a king is timid, the queen will doubt his right to rule, and she will challenge him. The lack of a strong king can send an entire herd into confusion, so much so that the order of dominance may be upset. Wild goats are unable to choose a queen from their numbers when this happens.

One of Sonny's favorite targets is the top strand of wire fencing surrounding his enclosure. He knows that Diane doesn't like him climbing it. If Sonny could put into words this act of piracy, he probably would hit the fence joyously and shout: "This will get her goat!" Diane always knows what Sonny is doing when she hears the squealing of wires and the popping of staples.

Sonny behaves like a film star in the lens of a camera. He knows he is handsome, and he loves attention. When the camera points in his direction, he raises his front legs to the top wire and strikes a proud pose.

Like most bucks on a dairy, he is isolated from the does. As long as Sonny can see the others, and they can come up to his fence, he doesn't mind. Being affectionate and bottle-raised, he loves everyone who visits him. The best time of day for him, now that he understands Diane, is when she comes to feed and talk to him.

Sonny

Czar

S onny looks on as the kids jump and stumble near his fence. They have excess energy after their long night of sleep. Speckles catches a leg on one of the wires. Since she is a kid that moves in several directions in one gambol, she frees herself after a moment of panic.

Czar comes to the fence and stands beside his pasture mate. He seems more interested in watching Sonny than the kids. Before being moved, Czar was alone in a small enclosure across the driveway. That territory was his and a place uncomplicated; he had no direct confrontations to endure; there was no order of dominance to trouble him.

Czar is an American Toggenburg born two years ago, and he came from a large herd. The handler was very busy and had little time to give individual attention. Czar was raised by his mother and taken off her just long enough to be disbudded and to have his ears tattooed. Both experiences were unpleasant for him, and because he had had little contact with humans, he distrusted them from then on.

If the handler could have spent time with Czar, there would have been fewer problems. Stroking and talking to a young goat will reduce shyness and suspicion. Such attention makes it easier on the kid when it is separated from the mother. In Czar's case this might have turned him around completely. The best time for establishing such closeness is at birth. The licking, nuzzling, and cleaning that does give their young increase the feeling of security, and with a human present, there is less chance of the newborn growing up wild—the handler's voice and smell becoming familiar at a time when the young animal is most sensitive to the world.

Czar was shy as a deer when he was shipped to the Dishner farm at the age of five and a half weeks. He was terrified of people and had the look of a creature loose in the wilds. After trying to feed Czar on the more impersonal Lambar feeder—a bucket with a wheel of nipples—Diane switched him to a bottle until weaning. Learning that his milk came directly from a human was the only thing that helped to make him less frightened of people.

Czar had every reason to find disbudding unpleasant. There is pain for the first few seconds, and goats are quite vocal about it. And why shouldn't they shout? The disbudding iron is more than a thousand degrees Fahrenheit.

Like goats in the wild, Czar would have found horns a useful weapon of defense. If he had been allowed to keep them, the dominance struggle would have been in his favor. Within the confines of a small dairy herd where animals enforce their own order through strength, horns are dangerous. A swift butt on the udder of a milker or a collision of two rambunctious bucks could cause serious injuries.

Disbudding should be done while the kids are very young—as soon as the horn tips can be felt. This is usually five to seven days in the Swiss breeds and up to two weeks in Nubians. Dehorning is more painful if the horns are allowed to grow. Some kids are naturally hornless, and they can be identified by the looser skin on the tops of their heads and straighter hair covering the horn spots. Disbudding is done when the skin is drawn tightly and the hair is curly over the buds.

Diane has never seen a hornless Nubian in her herd, but among the Toggenburgs this isn't unusual. She once had such a Toggenburg called Wisteria. When this doe had her first kids, three of them, the babies all had horns. The next time the doe kidded, triplets again, the kids were hornless.

Another necessary chore on a dairy, and possibly contributing to Czar's distrust of people, is tattooing. All goats must have tattoos if they are to be registered or entered in shows. The inside of the ear is the place where the tongs leave their marks except for the LaMancha—this breed is tattooed on the web of the tail. Most goat keepers place a breeder's tattoo in the goat's right ear and a number to identify the animal in the left. Kids are often numbered in the order of their birth, and this marking is done early on the newborns.

Then there is debleating. This experience could have plunged Czar below the emotional level of recovery and kept him forever in terror of humans. The practice isn't common on dairies, though it is sometimes done to silence noisy goats in populated areas. The veterinarian is called and an operation is performed on the goat's vocal chords. Afterwards, the animal is unable to make loud sounds, only gurgles or sedate bleats. All the goats keep their voices on the Dishner farm—the herd that Diane calls "Dubl Squeez." Their mistress thinks debleating is cruel and wouldn't have it done on any goat unless it were to keep peace within a neighborhood.

Sonny & Czar

9:40 a.m.

I t is now mid-morning. 9:40 a.m. The sun has scaled the highest
hillside, and only a few dense clumps of grass beyond the pasture
are jeweled with dew. The sound of logs being unloaded at the far
end of the wood products mill is partly muted by the March wind.
Hay is still being pulled from the racks in the goat barn, but the
pace is slower. Then a trampling noise and the dull thud of two
does placing well-aimed butts to settle some minor skirmish. A
bleat of outrage follows.

Tatiana appears in the doorway. Only her head and neck can
be seen clearly as she looks out. The sunlight catches the shimmer
of her hair, the brown and white and black markings along her
face. Her white ears hang like exotic leaves in the negative of some
photograph.

The kids dart in and out of the goat barn. Then slowly, one by
one, and by twos, both does and kids appear until the building has
been emptied. They stand in uneven knots of color by the water
trough. Hansel and Gretchen, now back with Tracy, walk along
the cleated plank that is used when the yard becomes muddy after a
long rain. Gretchen stops to look at her mother, and the twins
stand for a moment with their heads close together and their
shoulders touching. The does have had their fill of hay. It is time
now for greener forage. But first a cool drink of water and a look
around the yard before moving into the pasture.

After watching Tracy push the length of her body against a

rack and twist her head to pull hay—a way of blocking Giselle until Tracy has had her share—and seeing the others waste half the hay they pull, an observer would conclude that these goats with their poor table manners aren't particular in what they eat. But they are all fussy. They won't take a mouthful of hay that another has touched. Even a delicious apple will be rejected. Diane has bitten into one and offered the rest to the herd only to see them smell the fruit, look disgusted, and turn away.

Giselle and Kiaya are the last to lower their heads at the water trough. Adult does drink about a gallon a day and more if they are pregnant. If the weather is cold, they will drink less. But the water must be fresh. A thirsty goat will take only a few sips if the drinking supply is stale. After Giselle and Kiaya have satisfied their thirst, they join Wish and the others in the field.

Goats are browsers, not grazers. They like to pull down the things they eat, and they take delight in nibbling at anything left hanging. Clothes on a line aren't nutritious, but they can be tempting to a curious goat. Left to themselves in the wild, goats know what is good for them. It is when their food is supplied that they rely on the judgment of the handler who feeds them.

In the wild, they make their own decisions and never with uncertainty. If a plant should be in question, the queen doe approaches it carefully, sniffs the leaves, and takes a tiny nibble. Should she decide it isn't good, she spits it out, wipes her mouth on the grass, circles the plant, and shows fear and disgust. The buck has his own response to a questionable plant. He rears up like a warrior and tramples it until there is little left.

The belief that goats will devour anything has done much to damage their image. Prejudice and misinformation never seem to let up. The following—overheard at a fair—is a response that occurs all too frequently.

"Daddy," asks the little boy, "what kind of an animal is that? Is it a deer?"

The father laughs.

"My word, no, my boy! That's a goat."

"Why does your nose get all crooked and wrinkly?" asks the child who never runs out of questions.

"Goats are strange creatures," says the father. "They eat tin cans and all kinds of trash, climb up on buildings, and they are smelly."

"What makes them smell?"

"They just do."

"But why?"

"I don't know why, exactly," replies the father. "I guess because they are goats."

There have been many cartoons and stories about goats eating tin cans. Of course they don't eat metal! But since they are browsers and enjoy the bark from trees and most pulp products, they will chew the paper from cans. Often with disastrous results. Goat handlers try to keep all tin cans away from their herds as mouths can be cut badly on metal edges.

The natural curiosity of a goat and the flexibility of its lips have contributed to the myth that here is an animal willing to sample anything. When it comes to browsing not all authorities agree. One author on the subject stated that goats considered poison oak and ivy "manna from heaven." But veterinarian Samuel B. Guss, college professor and contributor to numerous behavioral articles on goats, thought otherwise. "I have never seen goats eat poison oak; I doubt that they would eat it unless there were nothing else to eat. They do not eat poison ivy without bad effect, and those who handle and milk them may really suffer from poison ivy."

Runaway goats in a garden will not identify oleander until it is too late—even if a herd is selective in what it eats. This plant is poisonous to them, and there are others which are harmful, such as rhododendron, azalea, mountain laurel, bracken fern, buttercup, cowslip, and lily-of-the-valley.

Because goats are ruminants (cud chewers with four-chambered stomachs) their diet is largely roughage. (We humans may think: What a waste of time—this business of sitting around part of a day chewing a cud! But if we had four stomachs and required a lengthy—and perhaps deeply thoughtful—period of digestion, one can only guess how different our world would be.) The best possible combination of roughage for goats is oats and alfalfa. The two complement one another, and with good hay goats will have sufficient fiber for a rumen activity.

Goat handlers can defend their animals when the tin can accusation is brought up. Not goats but cattle are the metal eaters. One of the large beef packing plants at one time had a mound of material taken from the stomachs of slaughtered cattle. The pile was seven feet high and with articles as odd as spark plugs and alarm clock bells.

Goats are not lawn mowers. Most of them will ignore grass when there is other roughage around. Alfalfa is the most popular feed for dairy goats in the United States. Either fresh or fed as hay, and it is a nutritious offering. Goats form habits in eating, and when it becomes necessary to change their feed it should be done gradually.

The Dishner pasture is adequate for the herd, though there is a shortage of brush. The pasture space is rotated during the growing season for regrowth. The goats prefer a broad leaf type of grasses and legumes. Alfalfa or alfalfa-mixed hay is fed to the milkers, and the favorite brush is a wild willow. They also like thimbleberry and salmonberry, in addition to blackberry leaves, blossoms, and berries. Diane doesn't keep a goat garden. If she did, two of the vegetables would be carrots and kale. Apples are sometimes offered as a special treat but in small amounts. A large serving of fruit can cause a goat to scour.

Tracy pushes the length of her body against the hayrack—a
way of blocking Giselle

Czar finishing his morning hay

11:00 a.m.

The morning is going rapidly. Nearly 11:00 a.m. There is no longer a chill in the air as a blanket of mist drags a small cloud behind a distant hillside. From the nearby mill yard, a log truck grinds out of neutral and leaves.

The goats are full after having had their hay and an hour of browsing in the pasture. They now are ready to search for places away from the sun. There they will lie down, chew their cud, and have their midday naps. Wish and Fawn wander toward the water trough for another drink and all the others follow.

Giselle is near the fence and away from the herd. She looks up and comes running. Suddenly, halfway along the cleated plank in the yard, she stops. She sees part of herself reflected in a small puddle of water. There is a look of surprise on her face as she sniffs the image. Giselle may be wondering if this is some new goat she must challenge to establish dominance.

Wish lowers her head and nibbles a taste of water before satisfying her thirst. Then she strolls to the gate and inspects the lock with her tongue. The bolt has been fastened securely, and she can tell in one lick that there is no hope of picking the lock with her teeth. She quickly gives up the thought of trying elsewhere. This is not the right time of day to escape the pasture. What she needs now is a cool place in the shade for her cud and nap.

Wish is five years old and a purebred Toggenburg. She is structurally sound with no noticeable weaknesses and should remain top doe for several more years. Her place in the dominance order hasn't always been first. She was number two for a time when the queen was a Nubian called Spice. Diane realized that Wish would take over immediately when Spice left the herd. Wish's desire to be boss was strong, and she was physically big enough to get her way.

The Dishners call Wish the "Burp Goat." She is incapable of sounding the usual Toggenburg cry; all she can do is emit a few indecisive grunting and burping noises. When Wish tells the others to keep out of her favorite sleeping place in the barn, she makes her demands known by two-thirds body language and one-third garbled bleats. She also makes the same feeble sounds during a head-on butting attack.

Wish was bottle-raised and enjoys being with people. She is curious about humans, even while making certain that a stranger poses no threat to the herd. One always finds Wish up front after an unexpected noise or motion. She is firm in her role of queen and unafraid. When Wish moves forward, assuring the others that all is well, they follow without hesitation.

Size, strength, and determination to become a leader are factors that crown a queen. An average-sized doe can become boss if she doesn't give in when challenged by the larger members of the herd. Wish came to the Dishner farm when she was two years old. Diane often wonders, had she been able to train her from the beginning, would this queen goat be less inclined to push the others about for personal satisfaction when in an aggressive mood.

Testing strength and bossing the next goat down in the dominance order goes on from Wish to Kiaya. It is an assessment hierarchy in which each goat recalls previous challenges, and the entire herd takes for granted that the top doe comes first and is favored. It is the queen that puts an end to squabbles and is the first to face danger when there is no king buck around to help her. In the wild, the lead goat may be a buck, but usually on a dairy, where the males and females are separated, it is the oldest or most aggressive doe. So intricate is the top doe's relationship with the other goats that they are unable to choose a queen if their handler prevents them from settling differences amongst themselves.

One new keeper of a small group of goats spent more time wrestling her does from the milk stand and into the pasture than milking them. After several days, the handler discovered the problem: the leader wasn't being milked first. When the order of dominance was observed, the other goats happily let down their milk and quickly joined their queen in the pasture. Even an experienced handler like Diane sometimes forgets, and when this happens she notices an immediate change in the herd. All the goats, from Wish to Kiaya, are upset.

A handler can lead a herd on range like a king buck. If the keeper should disappear behind some bush, the queen will look up worriedly and call. Should there be no answer, and the lead doe thinks they have been abandoned, she will take over the herd. This happens in a wooded area, but in open country the entire herd comes running in search of the handler.

In the wild, the king buck leads the herd with the queen beside him or close behind. The goats know just where to browse and what time of year is best for different foraging. The king nibbles at the upper branches of a bush while the queen pulls down several boughs for the smaller members before helping herself. When the queen decides to continue she looks at the king and bleats. He stops eating immediately and moves on with the others following in single file. After several such stops, the herd finds an area of mixed forage. There they lie down to chew their cud. They stay in this location until evening draws near. Then the king leads them to a sheltered area where they will spend the night. On the way, one of the older does or the queen may stop to nibble some leafy bush or bark of a tree. The king waits patiently, and the others stand by without eating.

Goats are more aggressive than sheep in a herd situation, and there may be differences in breeds of goats. In a mixed group of British animals, for example, it was observed that Toggenburgs showed more aggression than Saanens. The presence of horns, age and weight, plus determination, all help to decide leadership. One of the more dramatic displays of the dominance struggle occurs when a doe has been separated from a herd for several months and then is reintroduced. The queen ignores the returnee while some of the older and middle-placed does assert their order of dominance.

This once happened in a herd in which the mother of the returned goat stood aside and watched the struggle. After the head smashing and rump butting was over, and the other does had gone back to what they were doing before the challenges, the mother approached the daughter and nuzzled her. It was as if she wanted to comfort her grown-up child. But in some cases there is no sympathy as the mother and daughter fail to recognize each other.

"It is the tendency of the daughter of the herd queen to be boss of all her peers," replied Diane Dishner when asked if a determined doe or queen usually had a kid that grew to fill a strong position in the herd. "Wish is the queen of the adults and her daughter (Giselle) was queen of all her peers and younger ones."

"What about Fawn?" the mistress of Dubl Squeez was asked.

"Fawn is a year older. But Giselle is not far behind Fawn in aggressiveness. One day, I think Giselle may become queen. There is the possibility if her mother, Wish, is ever out of the picture."

"And what about Kiaya?" Diane was asked. "Why is this yearling lowest in the dominance order?"

"Because her mother (Cindra) is one of the lower adults. Kiaya got pushed around more as a kid because of Cindra's place in the herd. A queen's daughter learns her mother's ways and is protected from all the other mothers."

"Do you mean Tracy, the number two doe, wouldn't put Giselle in her place?"

Diane Dishner smiled.

"You don't touch the daughter of the queen, even if you are number two."

Giselle sees herself in a puddle of water

Wish, The Queen

Fawn and Giselle

11:30 a.m.

The herd is interrupted. 11:30 a.m. Naps must wait. Two vehicles enter the driveway by the barn, and the sound of doors slamming brings Wish to her feet. She leaves her cool resting place in the shadows and comes forward into the sunlight. Several strangers are advancing toward the gate, and the sun blinds Wish momentarily. Her ears are alert as she squints at the intruders. Then a familiar voice. The herd breaks formation instantly; no dominance order is needed now; they know there is nothing to fear when Diane is around.

Several adults and two girls are with their mistress. No introductions, polite conversations, and commentaries on the weather are expected in the goat world. To a bottle-raised kid and lover of humans like Speckles such behavior would be boring. She remembers Alex and David Jamshidnejad visiting the farm only the day before, and how she was able to lick Alex's chin as he struggled to hold her in his arms. Speckles is the first among the young ones to reach the gate.

The girls, Amber and April Smith, reach for Speckles the moment they are in the pasture, but the youngster is too excited and can't stop squirming. Instead, Amber scoops Tyrel into her arms. He struggles to nuzzle her face and suddenly changes his mind. He nibbles her clothing, half-deciding that here is something good to eat.

April picks up Tania to stroke her. Tatiana begins to worry and comes over to see if all is well with her baby. After the mother has licked one of Tania's ears, much to April's amusement, Tat turns her attention to Tyrel. He has wiggled away from Amber and is now sniffing one of April's boots.

It is impossible to hold Speckles for long—her head twisting, legs pumping, entire body quivering. Hansel and Gretchen aren't as comfortable as Conrad and Clover when the Smith girls try to hold them. A wariness is present whenever they are picked up.

There is too much activity in the yard for Fawn and Giselle: two giggling girls, adult humans they don't know, a man jumping about with a black box that makes a threatening growl and click, the photographer's wife going from one doe to another in fear that some will not get their share of attention, a strutting bantam trying to perch on the nearest human head, and seven kids darting crazily in every direction. Fawn's and Giselle's body language is saying: This is no place for Toggenburgs! The two disappear into the barn, and after several long moments they peek from the doorway.

Tracy, too, has had enough. She marches away with Hansel and Gretchen close behind. Then the twins scamper along the edge of the pasture and begin sniffing and rooting around a partly chewed log. They rub their bodies against the uneven surface of knots before trying to climb up. They already are playing the game of climbing steep slopes like grown-up wild goats.

Studies have determined the first few minutes after a birth to be the critical period for does to form attachments to their kids. If the newborns are taken from their mothers at birth and the does are not given the chance of licking and nuzzling, the kids may be rejected by their dams. A total rejection can occur within an hour.

The new mother gives a short, low-pitched bleat to call her newborn, and sometimes she will begin calling before the birth occurs. This bleat is used to get the baby's attention and also to communicate with one of her older kids. The newborn, however, isn't drawn to its mother as much as the dam to her baby. Small as it is, weighing only four to eight pounds at birth, the new kid is up and jumping about in minutes and will go toward any large moving object. A baby goat is very impressionable, and the first few hours of its life may well influence the kind of animal it will be later when interacting with the herd. If the handler is there to comfort and assist the dam, a bonding will be established, and the kid will look upon the human as a second mother.

Most handlers prefer being around at the time of birth, not only for the sake of bonding but to provide the dam with extra nourishment. Does lose body fluids during birthing, and one popular drink to serve is warm water with molasses. The warmth of the water comforts the new mother, and the molasses gives an extra boost of sugar energy.

Soon, the newborn is ready to nurse, and that meal will be the most important one of its life. During the first four days of nursing, the mother's milk is rich in colostrum; milk that is yellow, thick, sticky, and containing antibodies and proteins that help fight diseases. Without this feeding of colostrum, the baby has little chance of reaching adulthood. Newborns should have this milk within a half hour of birth and no later than the first day.

A kid is born with the same sensitivity as a single-stomached animal. The first three chambers of the digestive system aren't developed to full rumen capability at birth. Until these three other stomachs are functional, the kid can only digest milk. But within a week young goats are imitating their dams—nibbling hay, drinking water, tasting grain, and visiting the mineral lick. Many handlers encourage kids by offering them small-leaved branches. Ash is a big favorite.

When a kid is to be bottle-fed at Dubl Squeez, it is separated from the mother for six weeks. This is often done when the young goat is four days old. The baby is placed where the mother can see it but not within reach of her udder. Should the kid begin nursing again, the six-week separation would start all over.

Bottle-fed kids grow faster when their milk is served at body temperature. Baby goats drink from 2 to 10 ounces in the beginning, and before the first month is over they will be averaging a pint of milk 4 times a day. These four feedings continue until the twelfth week. The kids will be consuming other foods at this time, and the amount of milk can be decreased.

In many domestic herds, weaning begins when the handler sees that the doe is tired of nursing. A kid doesn't need milk after 2 to 3 months. If the milk supply slackens or the baby is too rough with its teeth, the dam will begin the weaning herself. At this time the grain feeding begins in earnest. A high protein mix is a kid's first meal of grain at Dubl Squeez.

When Hansel and Gretchen were old enough to leave the barn for the first time, they appeared quite timid and didn't have much to do with the herd. But gradually they began paying more attention to the adult does. As babies, they must learn not to nurse the wrong dam and to avoid teasing the bigger goats.

In the wild, dams find hiding spots for their young and avoid visiting these places except when nursing the kids. Isolating them not only protects the youngsters from predators but from aggressive adults in the herd. Many handlers on dairies where quarters are crowded provide boxes for the kids to hide in during these early days.

Development is swift. The first signs of aggressiveness occur when the kids are around 7 to 10 days old. These are mock battles; play fights of rearing, butting, and pushing. Such engagements are not serious enough to establish any order of dominance among the younger members of the herd, but they do establish behavior patterns.

The does at Dubl Squeez have their young in the early spring. Diane believes that kids born at this time of year grow faster because there are fewer bacteria flourishing and greener more nutritious choices for the kids after weaning. Hansel and Gretchen already are beginning to act like mature little goats, and they increasingly are curious when visiting the more likely places for browsing at the far end of the pasture.

These Toggenburg twins are too shy by nature to jump on visitors who try to stroke them. Kids are so much fun to play with, but they grow quickly, and when a goat is no longer allowed to jump up affectionately because of its size, the animal feels neglected. This will never be a problem for Hansel and Gretchen, but it may be for Speckles.

What Speckles doesn't know is that she will have a good home when she is old enough to leave the Dishner farm. She has been adopted by the Smith family, and her mistresses will be Amber and April. Speckles became an orphan because she was the smallest of triplets born to a yearling. It is rather unusual to have three babies for a first kidding. The mother didn't have enough milk for such a family, and Diane volunteered to take over Speckles' bottle feedings.

Speckles

Hansel and Gretchen

Gretchen

Clover & Conrad (top)

Tyrel and Tania

Fawn's and Giselle's body language is saying: This is
no place for Toggenburgs! The two disappear into
the barn, and after several long moments they peek
from the doorway.

April picks up Tania to stroke her. Tatiana begins to worry. Meanwhile, Tyrel is sniffing one of April's boots.

Amber Smith with Tyrel and Clover

Clover & Conrad

Gretchen

Tania & Conrad

12:15 p.m.

It is 12:15 p.m. The humans have left. The herd is resting now after all the excitement. The kids are beside their dams, and every goat has found a cool place at the edge of the pasture. Fawn shares a small circle of shade with Tracy and her twins. They all lie with their front legs tucked under, eyes closed, heads nodding in and out of sleep, and short tails twitching lazily at insects.

Tracy is a five-year-old American Toggenburg. She has been on the Dishner farm longer than any of the other does—arriving when she was a year and a half old. She has a good disposition and is very certain of her position just behind Wish. If Tracy were taken away for several weeks and then returned to the herd, they all would remember her. There might be a little dominance difficulty with number three doe, Tatiana, filling number two place, but the argument would be settled quickly, and Tracy would continue as number two goat.

Tracy has had seven kids, all of them twins except for a single baby from her first kidding, and usually they are females. Having baby girls in the goat world is just the luck of the draw for Tracy as the sire determines the sex of the kids.

Hansel and Gretchen couldn't ask for a better mother. Tracy watches them closely, doesn't allow the other does to shove them aside roughly, and when the twins wander too far into the field, she either calls or hurries to join them.

Tracy looks shorter and gets dirtier than the other goats. This is because she has such short legs. During the winter when her coat is longer she'll get mud on her belly. In dry season there are no problems—unless she decides that the steaming manure heap is a good mattress for an afternoon nap. Her present difficulty is in keeping her weight while suckling her babies. Because she is such an attentive mother the twins are often demanding to be fed.

It is no accident that Fawn has settled close to Tracy like another kid instead of an adult companion. To Fawn, Hansel and Gretchen are nuisances.

For the past two years, Diane has allowed the does to raise their own babies, and the kids have been separated temporarily from their mothers after five months. Fawn, the dam-raised daughter of Tracy, was brought up this way.

After being away from Tracy during the weaning period, Fawn returned, and both mother and daughter remembered one another immediately. Then Tracy gave birth again, and the babies took up most of her attention. No dam wants a yearling daughter too close to her new kids.

There was confusion at first, and Fawn was jealous. She couldn't understand why these tiny outsiders were being favored. Whenever Fawn could, she would give her mother's new babies a shove or butt to assert what she felt was her rightful place in the family circle. When this happened, Tracy would turn on Fawn as if to say: You get away!

There was nothing the yearling daughter could do but keep her distance and appear agreeable. After incidents of jealousy and confrontation, Tracy, Fawn, and the twins could be seen in the pasture together like a contented family group.

Goats can be jealous of one another, but they don't hold grudges for long. They prefer to settle differences among themselves and to live in harmony. If two does are at odds longer than usual, the other goats will try to get between the feuding pair to stop the fighting. For bossy goats that squabble all too frequently, some handlers, as a temporary measure of restraint, resort to a nineteen-thirty chain-gang tactic—the use of a leg hobble to limit aggression.

Like Giselle, Fawn is shy and accepts Diane as a sort of care-taker or boss herd mate. Fawn looks upon all other humans as suspicious characters on her home grounds, even Lyle Dishner, and she sees him several times a week.

It is unlikely that Fawn will ever be top doe. She has Giselle's present shyness and isn't aggressive enough to win dominance. Fawn sees Giselle as a threat to her place in the herd. (When one is third from the last in a group of seven does, and the next to last goat is threatening to step up in the world, one should worry.) The competition became noticeable to Fawn shortly after Giselle's weaning. The two soon were at odds, and Fawn began pushing Giselle around in the barn whenever they were close together.

Brought up in the Dishner herd, Giselle was raised by Wish and had limited contact with Diane in the early weeks. Giselle is suspicious of people and doesn't like being touched. From the rear of the herd, she looks shyly at all intruders, and one expects her to rush off at any moment.

But within the group, Giselle has a boldness and is learning to defend herself. Already she has acquired some domineering techniques and practices them on Kiaya, the last in the dominance order. Like Kiaya and Fawn, Giselle was separated from her mother and reunited after the weaning. Giselle bosses Kiaya around at mealtime, but the curly Nubian doesn't seem to mind. The two were close friends as babies, and they continue to be friends in and out of the barn.

Because she was so dependent on her mother, it took Giselle longer to accept Diane. Probably the one thing that is making Giselle more outgoing is the feeding of treats. Like all the others in the herd, she loves these daily protein pellets.

Since Giselle is only a yearling, she hasn't learned to behave properly when treats are shared. Like Fawn, she has the bad habit of jumping up when the pellets are brought out. There is no shyness then. Because Giselle and Fawn are young and still growing, they must get their heads above the larger does to have a chance at their shares.

Fawn

Tracy

INTERMISSION

It is 1:00 p.m. The herd is still resting at the edge of the pasture. Only Cindra appears awake as she lazily worries her cud. Shadows that were crouching at the base of trees at midday are just beginning to stretch themselves. There is a lull at the nearby wood products mill—not a workman in sight. This is a good time of day to go elsewhere; a time of intermission; a chance for the person writing these words to step away and to look back.

My first goat was Lucretia.

One afternoon while working for a small Maine town as a bookkeeper and property assessor, I heard a commotion in the hallway next to the office where I was punching a long column of figures into an adding machine. Too busy to get up and see what was going on, I kept to my task until I felt someone staring at me. Another complaining taxpayer I thought as I turned in my chair.

One doesn't expect to see a goat standing hoof-deep in the plush wall-to-wall carpeting of an office. But there Lucretia was, a small yearling of mixed breed, a curious scrub with one ear partly raised and bent and the other hanging in Nubian fashion. Her black-brown head was tilted to one side as she looked me over with her incredible brown-green eyes.

"A goat!" I said aloud. And then I felt foolish because I sounded like an usher at some grand occasion of state where a dignitary or monarch was making an entrance.

I heard giggles in the hallway, and the office secretary and her son peeked around the corner of the door. They were driving by with Nanny and thought it would be amusing to startle me with their recently-purchased pet.

There are too many goats answering to the names of Nanny and Billy, and here was another one. The yearling had been found at a livestock auction, and they never realized that looking after a goat was so much work. That was why the doe was going to a local dealer—unfortunately a man who had no sensitivity for the animals he bought and sold.

I often show little common sense when acquiring farm animals and pets. I've brought home thirteen cats in my time, three dogs, and once when living in a hotel I had a pet alligator. I usually get my animals just before taking long trips or when our surroundings are not ideal for adoptions. My wife and I already had gone through our farming stage with five pigs, one sheep, three hundred laying hens, rabbits, hamsters, bantams, and fifty roosters. But how could I let this yearling scrub be delivered into the hands of such an unfeeling man? Within minutes, I was the keeper of a goat.

Nanny was given the name Lucretia the moment I got her home. She was such a friendly animal and a delight to take on a leash when we went for walks. But there was a problem. Lucretia would begin bleating as soon as she was left alone, and we couldn't understand why she was so fussy. After consulting a husbandry book, my wife and I decided that the yearling needed company. The little doe had looked upon our dog, Spock, with some misgivings when she arrived, but they soon became friendly and the bleating stopped the moment the two were hitched outside together,

Spock kid-sat until the purchase of a purebred Saanen. This doe was milking a gallon a day when we got her, and one couldn't ask for a better goat than Angel. She had a calm disposition, was easy to look after, and what I especially liked about her was that she didn't bleat. (Evidently, a "burp goat" like Wish.) Lucretia was delighted to have one of her own kind around, and the two got along splendidly.

All was tranquil until my next impulsive act. A woodsman in

town asked if I would take over his Toggenburg doe. It was understood that he would get her back if there should be a problem. Why not? I thought. One more wouldn't make that much of a difference. Then foolishly, without looking her over first, I concluded the transaction with a handshake.

"Here comes Heidi!" the woodsman shouted as the Toggenburg squeezed herself out of the fender-battered coupe. The light chocolate-colored doe looked bigger than a yearling heifer as she alighted, stretched, and surveyed the dooryard. My mind immediately began playing tricks on me, and I was face to face with a suspicious hippo. Then I saw the horns and the tropical riverbank faded and I was in a Madrid bullring waving my matador's cape. "The chain comes with her," the man chuckled as he looped a section around my wrist. "Heidi's a real pussycat," he assured me, "and she loves to wrestle!"

The woodsman and his wife had spoiled the Toggenburg. The goat was ready to maul the first human in sight to show how much she cared. If one ignored her, she would nudge that cold-hearted person with her massive horns and insist on a wrestling match. I didn't drag her to and from the barn; she galloped me back and forth.

I should have taken all three goats into the open pasture and allowed them time to establish their order of dominance, but her horns troubled me. The way the Toggenburg lunged at the Saanen when they were next to each other in stalls convinced me that Angel could be injured seriously if the two were loose in the barn.

I pastured Lucretia and Angel in one field and Heidi in another. The longer the two adult does were kept apart, the more noticeable their frustration and animosity. Angel's milk production fell and much of Heidi's energy was spent in accosting Angel.

Lucretia witnessed the proceedings with her bent ear aslant and eyes shining with curiosity. She sensibly kept out of the squabble, but I could see that Heidi's explosive butts against the wall of the stall impressed the scrub. I didn't realize the extent of Lucretia's admiration until I noticed that she had taken on one of the big Togg's mannerisms.

When Heidi was a spoiled-rotten kid and the center of attention, which included a family circle of cats, dogs, and human kids, the woodsman and his wife would approach Heidi, tilt their heads to one side and say: "Oh what a pretty girl!" And Heidi would cock her head too. Soon, the Toggenburg was twisting her neck and tilting her head whenever she was stroked or when she felt attention should be coming her way. This habit fascinated Lucretia, and in no time she was doing a magnificent imitation. We now had two goats in our barn declaring themselves pretty girls.

Then one rainy day when the goats were in their stalls and we were away for several hours, Heidi managed to break down the partition. The poor Saanen had no place to stand her ground, and the skirmish must have been vicious. I found Angel bleeding from a gash on the side of her face, she had a chewed ear, and her udder was bruised and swollen. Heidi was back in her stall and looking thoroughly pleased with herself. I washed Angel, sterilized the cuts, and rubbed ointment on the bruises. Battered as she looked, her injuries were superficial.

The decision to return Heidi to her former home was a difficult one. I knew that I had failed as a handler because of my timidity, and I felt both sadness and relief as I watched the Toggenburg settle herself in the battered coupe for her ride back to familiar surroundings. Then as I turned away, I asked myself: Why do I get so involved? Our family would have been ahead financially if we bought our eggs and milk at the supermarket. But we would have missed the satisfaction of caring for our farm animals and the joy of watching them. And so I purchased another Saanen. Her name was Courtney and she came from the same herd as Angel.

The two Saanens recognized one another, and all went well until Lucretia grew jealous of Courtney. The small scrub began chasing the newcomer in the pasture, and in a very ungoatlike way, Courtney wouldn't defend herself. She would run off in a panic, bleating loudly. Angel sided with Courtney and turned on Lucretia. The new goat's bleating increased until it even got on Angel's nerves. Then the noisy Saanen was being chased by both goats. In and out of the pasture, poor Courtney kept crying for help. "Do something!" she seemed to be shouting from the open window of the barn.

A barking dog, the squeak of a weathervane, and loud music are sounds that I have come to dislike. After listening to Courtney for several weeks, the bleat of a frantic goat was being added to the list. I think somewhere in her there was buried that placid Saanen disposition. Courtney loved to be with people, she was an excellent milker, and she was easy enough to handle. It was her loud mouth that wearied us all.

I tried everything to shut her up. She was isolated, disciplined, placed in the same stall with Lucretia and then with Angel, she was rewarded with special treats, and given attention. But she kept complaining, steadily and nerve-rackingly. I was tempted to trick the first gullible stranger into taking her—preferably someone on a trip to a far country. Finally, after weeks of bleating, Courtney settled down and the cycle of caprine irritation was broken, though she remained a noisy goat.

Then, the way it so often happens when people decide to have goats, we came to that point when the decision was made not to have them. Our lives had taken another turn and our interests had drifted from the farm and centered elsewhere.

An ad in a local newspaper brought a kindly woman to our door who loved animals. She had never kept goats but it had been one of her lifelong ambitions. The woman was recently retired and wanted something to keep her thoroughly occupied. I said to myself: Lady do I ever have the goat for you! She purchased Angel and Courtney at bargain prices, and then I turned to her and said: "We can't sell Lucretia, but if you like, we'll give her to you."

The little scrub with the bent ear contentedly crawled into the back of the woman's station wagon between placid Angel and bleating Courtney. We watched the three goats go out the driveway and down the road. The last of our farm animals and a way of life worth remembering.

Wish, the number one goat

Tracy, the number two goat

Sonny

Alex Jamshidnejad with Conrad

Giselle

April Smith with Kiaya

Alex with Speckles

Wish

Fawn and Tatiana

Hansel

2:00 p.m.

The afternoon advances. 2:00 p.m. Tyrel is now awake. He runs from the barn and nearly collides with a bantam. The little Nubian is lucky it isn't Black Bart. They both pull back in surprise and stare at each other. The expression on both faces is clear: What kind of creature is this? Tyrel sniffs the clucking heap of feathers and decides that he wants nothing to do with it.

The does scatter at the far end of the pasture. They seem more spirited after their naps, quite ready for whatever adventures that may come. And this is the time of day when attempts are made to escape the browsing area in order to feast on untouched greens and bushes. Should Wish be the one to discover an opening, all the others would follow their queen.

If there is a way of untangling wires with a shove or unlatching a gate with a well-aimed butt, goats will find it. Any barricade less than four feet in height can be scaled. Most keepers learn early that it is necessary to place all latches on the outside of gates. Goats are able to pick locks with their teeth and slip open bolts with their noses. Sonny isn't the only one hard on fences. They all like to stand with their front hooves on the top wire or rail, and if they can sag or break down a barrier, they will do so with mischievous delight. These creatures are burglars; geniuses at solving the mysteries of locks. One handler had a buck so clever in escaping fences that he nicknamed the animal Hairy Houdini.

Goats also have a sense of humor. They enjoy getting loose

and misbehaving when their keeper's back is turned. These animals know very well when they are naughty. Their eyes will flicker with amusement while they peek around corners to see if they have been found out. Like small children, goats get bored quickly, and when this happens, the time for mischief is fast approaching. Some handlers try to prevent this by having a variety of toys for them to play with, such as tires to butt, ramps to climb, and platforms to stand on. But clever as they are, with the ability to adjust their lives to the many whims and quirks of different keepers, goats make poor circus animals. They aren't good at performing tricks.

They seem to be so human at times with their curiosity, greed, pride, and individuality. But we are wrong and do them a disservice when we make comparisons. Goats are goats the world over; they are never people; they are presences living and reacting differently and in their own ways. Too often, we blame them for their habits. Hector, the family dog, doesn't chew the rosebush or rip dear old Uncle Ambrose's long underwear from the clothesline. But Hector isn't a browser. He has his own doggie bowl and treats in the cupboard and a basket to sleep in at night. Horses and cows aren't allowed on the lawn and then punished for trampling the nearby bed of pansies. Goats, too, need their own space, a strong and high fence, and a keeper who is ready to give them care and understanding.

This day the herd is out of luck. There isn't one flaw in the fence that can lead them to better browsing. Kiaya and her mother, Cindra, approach each other by the wires. There is still a closeness, even though Cindra has twins dividing her attention. The two touch noses before moving off in different directions.

By the gate, a sudden explosion. It's Tatiana. She has been startled by something. The other does look at Wish to read her reaction. But the queen knows that Tat scares easily and there is no reason for alarm.

Tatiana, the number three doe, is a four-year-old, bottle-raised Nubian. She is affectionate and loves being around people. Very shy, she must become well-acquainted with visitors before feeling comfortable with them.

Dairy animals like Tat have English milking stock ties. English goats were crossed with those of African- and Oriental-Nubian origins. It was in 1883 that the first purebreds were imported to England from Paris. The name Anglo-Nubian was recognized as a breed in 1896, and fifteen years later several of these goats were shipped to America. Dairy operators frequently refer to them as the Jersey cow of milk goats.

Nubians are a gentle breed, though they can be stubborn, and their temperaments vary. If a stranger comes into the barn, Tatiana will peek in at the door and then run to the pasture. And when it is necessary for Diane to discipline her, Tat's ears will come up and she will panic. Cindra is more trusting and self-assured and quickly understands when her keeper corrects her.

The yearling Kiaya and the kid Speckles are examples of how differently Nubians are colored. Kiaya's two light-tan streaks near her eyes completely overpower the trusting and innocent look she has when she turns her black-brown head to see what Wish and the other does are doing. Speckles is so spotted that she becomes a jumble of tan, red, and creamy white colors as she stumbles after people with the hope that someone will pick her up.

Like most goats, Nubians can't stand to be left alone. If Tatiana and Cindra were the only two on the farm and one of them wandered out of sight, the alarm would be sounded. Some handlers describe the breed as restless, but Diane doesn't agree. She thinks her Nubians are the easy-going members of the herd. Then, pausing for a moment, she adds: "But they do show a loud mouth at times!"

The Nubian does, particularly Cindra and sometimes Tatiana, have a more soulful look than the Toggenburgs—Fawn and Giselle stare back in mild surprise, as if they were deer about to run off and hide in a thicket. Tat and Cindra haven't lost their Indo-Egyptian beginnings, and this becomes apparent when they are in a herd mixed with Toggs. The Nubians at Dubl Squeez seem more firmly influenced by gravitational pulls—less buoyant, and they somehow lack the alpine agility of the Toggenburgs when reacting to an unexpected noise or sudden motion.

If Tat had more confidence in herself, she probably would replace Tracy as number two goat. Of the Nubians, she is Diane's "least favorite," though the two are getting along better now that Tatiana knows what is expected of her. Being easily spooked and bleating loudly are among Tat's failings.

Tatiana is fortunate in having a mistress who understands the importance of discipline and regularity. With an indecisive handler, Tat might well suffer from stress. Many goats are unable to endure the smallest change in their daily routine; some are even suspicious when a hayrack or water trough has been moved slightly.

The goats on the Dishner farm have a minimum of stress in their lives. Like all dairy animals, they have the unpleasant experiences of weaning, disbudding, going to shows, and the occasional surgery performed by the veterinarian. Most of the stress at Dubl Squeez occurs when a new goat is introduced. This is particularly noticeable among those low in the dominance order. They get nervous about losing what position they have in the herd.

Tatiana has backed away from the gate. She hasn't been able to calm her fears. There still may be something dangerous nearby. What if Wish and the others are wrong? When asking herself such a question, Tat has a way of sticking her nose in the air, as if she were trying to smell what is threatening her before she runs off.

Tatiana

Mr. Peabody's Cow's Milk

Ed Robinson, an author and goat keeper, once was invited to give a luncheon talk before the Lions Club in Bridgeport, Connecticut. The setting was the main dining room of the fashionable Stratfield Hotel. To everyone's surprise, Robinson led in one of his does, milked her before the audience, and then had fifty of the men compare fresh goat's milk and warmed cow's milk. The response was predictable: one third guessed right, a third thought the cow's milk was from the goat, and the rest decided that the goat's milk was from a cow.

The biggest difficulty dairy goat operators have in successfully promoting their product is that they must convince the general public that the two milks taste about the same. Most shoppers are locked into buying habits when marching up and down the aisles of supermarkets. They take from the shelves foods they know, and only occasionally will they try something exotic. Goat's milk may be consumed by more than half of the world's population, but in the United States only five percent of the people have tried it.

Much of the prejudice against goat's milk begins in childhood. Parents think only of the cow when they consider a wholesome, traditional drink for their children. And so do most English nursery rhymes. Tommy knows that goats are fun to watch, but Papa has told him not to go near old Billy Buck because the animal has B.O. And Aunt Agatha has told Sue the story of how a picturesque old peasant offered Auntie a warm bowl of goat's milk when she was touring the Middle East. The goat had a dirty udder and the man's hands were just caked with grime.

Milk will have an odor if a doe is kept near a buck. This is the reason why dairy operators never allow the male to run with the herd. Odors are quickly absorbed by the milk, and when a goat eats foods that have volatile oils, the oils are released in the digestive tract and diffused throughout the body. Since vast amounts of blood are carried to the udder, some of these oils will pass into the milk. There are many things in a pasture that can affect the flavor—even fresh green grass can give an off-taste. If there is the presence of wild garlic or onion, the milk will taste like a dip for crackers. Juniper makes the milk taste like a mouthwash, but clover gives a flavoring of honey.

The following prank never loses its popularity among goat handlers.

It had been a sultry afternoon, and the unexpected visitors who had called on Mr. Peabody were about to leave.

"I'm sure glad you folks could stop by and look at my girls," said Peabody. "Not everyone wants to brave that dusty back road to get up here."

It wasn't the old man's daughters that the middle-aged couple had come to see but a small herd of French Alpines. Mr. Peabody lived alone on a farm at the top of a mountain.

"We don't have many goats in Cleveland," explained the woman, "and when the postmaster in your little village happened to mention your herd it seemed a fun way of ending our vacation."

"Something different," the husband added. "We can't sit in the sun on the resort's lawn all day, and fishing the lake for hours gets rather boring."

"What a poor host am I!" cried Peabody rising from his chair. "Let me get you good people something cool to drink."

"That would be truly wonderful," replied the woman. "I am somewhat parched."

"We can't have that," Mr. Peabody chuckled. "How about a

refreshing glass of goat's milk?"

"Oh my, oh no!" they both cried out.

"Not goat's milk?"

The old man pretended to be puzzled.

The couple exchanged glances and looked uncomfortable. Then the husband, deciding that the truth was better than a lie, spoke up.

"We don't want to hurt your feelings, Mr. Peabody, but Angie and me don't much care for the taste."

The host wasn't at all insulted.

"Perhaps a cool glass of cow's milk?"

"That would be delightful!" replied the woman. Both she and her husband were obviously relieved.

Peabody went to the refrigerator and poured them tall glasses of milk from a milk carton that was labeled *Wentworth Dairy*.

"I get my cow's milk from Al Wentworth," explained the goat keeper. "He has a fine herd of Jerseys."

The host placed the glasses of milk before his guests and then served himself some milk from a different container.

"I'll stick with the goat's milk," he told them. "But I do understand your reluctance. Not everyone enjoys the taste."

The couple upended their glasses in chugalug fashion.

"One can always tell good old cow's milk," the woman commented after wiping her mouth with a handkerchief.

"We don't have Jerseys like that in Cleveland," said the husband. "That sure hits the spot!"

Mr. Peabody was well pleased with himself as he escorted the couple to their automobile and waved good-bye. The trick always worked and it gave him so much pleasure. What he couldn't understand was the gullibility of visitors. Why on earth should a keeper of milking goats waste one penny on a carton of cow's milk?

Fawn, watching Tracy and the twins

Wish, chewing her cud

3:15 p.m.

The afternoon shadows are stretching themselves into grotesque shapes. 3:15 p.m. The herd stands by the water trough. Giselle turns to peer through the wire fence at Czar. She has a way of lifting her head slowly and arching her neck gracefully. Sonny, wanting to be noticed, rears up on the fence and scratches his head on a rope lashed to the roof of a shelter. This is nervous displacement and is practiced at times by most living creatures. Tracy, unable to quench an earlier thirst, lowers her head to the trough and drinks deeply as the twins begin nursing.

A vehicle enters the drive by the barn. One look and they all know. Diane is back! The herd comes running as she looks to see if anyone is missing. She is in luck this day. There are no escapees to round up or fences to repair.

Cindra reaches the gate before the others, but Sonny gets attention first. His front legs are on the wires once more, and there is a metallic choir of squeals and groans.

Finally, Cindra hears her name called. She is one of the friendliest of goats and delights in being stroked. She has blossomed into a milker and is keeping up in production with Tracy—an accomplishment for a Nubian. Cindra is number four in the dominance order. Long-legged and less inclined to get dirty during the rainy season, she is a big, rangy goat, a lot like Tatiana in appearance. Calmer than Tat, and more capable of handling herself in emergencies, Cindra isn't placid always; she gets extremely nervous before birthing.

A human looking at Cindra might think: I'm lucky to be what I am! Who would want to be a goat? If Cindra could use our language to answer such a question, she probably would reply: "I do, and I want nothing more!" Yes, of course, says the human more doubtful than ever. But isn't your sort of life dull and meaningless?

A talkative Cindra would respond: "The cool taste of water on a warm day, the smell of fresh hay in the rack, and that scoop of grain while I'm letting down my milk—these are only a few of the pleasures and comforts. I have a mistress who cares for me, and there are the kids. I can nap when I like, and I have time for my cud." Then with a goatlike gleam, Cindra concludes: "not forgetting Sonny!"

Yes, yes, mutters the human, impatient as a parent with a prattling daughter, but what about the bad things?

"Like you, we have our miseries," Cindra replies. "I hate getting wet, and my hooves must be trimmed more often than anyone's in the herd! Not to mention the real horrors that still go on—one hears rumors—such as debleating and being shipped to a keeper one can't stand. And there are the ordinary, everyday ills and aches from birthing, disbudding, going to shows, weaning, and bloating . . . ."

Gruesome indeed, the human interrupts. I'm lucky to be what I am. But Cindra now is bored. All she can do is shake her head and advise: "I would ruminate on that if I were you!"

The trimming of hooves is done every four to six weeks on the Dishner farm, and the kids get their first trim when they are about four months old. Hooves grow quickly. In the wild, goats wear them down by walking on uneven ground and climbing steep slopes.

Keepers want their show animals to look sleek. This means haircuts and baths. Being washed is a humiliating, uncomfortable experience for goats. When it starts to rain, which is often in Oregon, the Dubl Squeez herd runs for the barn. They may go out in the rain to get a drink of water from the trough, but they come back galloping.

This dislike of getting wet is sometimes used as a way of disciplining goats. One handler, who had a doe that bleated all the time, fired a squirt gun whenever the animal had too much to say. Better this method than debleating, reasoned the keeper, and kinder. Within days, the doe was making only a squeak followed by the ducking of her head in anticipation of another volley of water.

It is difficult to keep goats clean when a yard is muddy after a long rain. Hair on the bellies and udders must be clipped and bellies brushed for more sanitary conditions at the milk stand. Goats seem to enjoy this grooming, and during the summer they can withstand the heat better with less hair.

Another chore on a dairy is the provision of bedding. Many handlers prefer sawdust to straw because it is more absorbent, but in Oregon this is difficult to find. Diane likes to bed her stalls with three to four inches of sawdust topped with old grass hay or straw. Some keepers provide sleeping benches off the floor, but the Dishner herd is given lots of fluffy bedding so they can shape it to their liking.

The mistress of Dubl Squeez looks uneasily at Sonny Beige's fence. She expects to see more loose staples since morning and particularly after so many visitors. Pleased to find no damage, she backs out of the drive for home.

Giselle wanders up to the fence to see if Czar and Sonny have left hay in their rack. She accidentally gets too close to Fawn. The action is swift and predictable. Fawn isn't going to be nudged by an upstart goat! She turns on Giselle, rears, and delivers a well-timed blow on the rump. A bleat of surprise comes from Giselle, and Fawn turns away pleased with herself.

Sonny, wanting to be noticed, rears up on the fence and
scratches his head on a rope lashed to the roof of a shelter

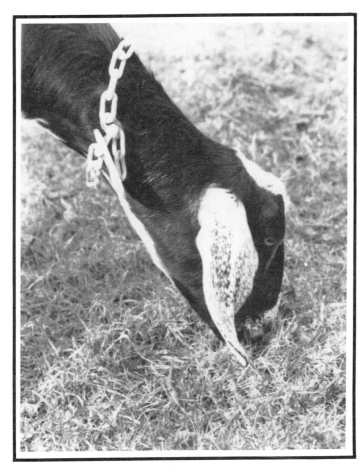

Cindra

4:30 p.m.

The younger kids are asleep in the barn. 4:30 p.m. The afternoon is nearly over. It is still too early for Hansel and Gretchen to be separated from Tracy for the night, but the mother has had enough for now. They have been after her all day. She leads them to the barn hoping that they will sleep. The twins are at Tracy's heels, their little tails and ears erect as they try to keep in step with their dam.

Kiaya slips loose from the protective knot of the other does and wanders to the fence where Sonny and Czar are standing. The two bucks watch her, their eyes wide, expecting approval, but several threads of hay dangling from their rack have captured her attention. Kiaya twists her dark head through the wires and pulls free a few spears, dropping half while trying to decide if this is stale hay.

One wouldn't think that Kiaya was brought up by her dam. She is like a bottle-raised kid around people. Mild by nature, Kiaya is a purebred Nubian. She is a large goat for her age, and when fully grown may surpass her mother, Cindra, in the dominance order. From the beginning, Kiaya's love of people was noticeable. Her dark eyes glowed whenever Diane or visitors were close by. But these expressions of warmth often were overlooked because of the startling light-tan markings of color near both her eyes.

Kiaya doesn't like cameras and feels threatened whenever she hears the whine of a lens. She moves behind Wish and the others for protection. There may be few advantages in being last in the dominance order, but this is one of them. Let her look out for me she seems to be saying as she nudges behind the shoulder of a more experienced doe.

One would think that beautiful rangy Kiaya would take delightful snapshots. She is such a remarkable goat in appearance in the sunlight, but the two tan markings by her eyes look like granny glasses in need of repair. Her warm brown and black colors lose contrast in black and white photographs.

Kiaya's love for people and her acceptance of Diane as a boss and member of the herd never change. She is a trusting and loyal animal and content with her domestic habitat. But there is another side to gentle Kiaya; a part of her that would forsake the dairy and all her human friends. It is something that all goats share: that desire to be free and wild again.

When a goat herd is sent out to pasture and allowed to roam unattended for several weeks, the group becomes wild and looks upon their handler as the enemy. The need to depend upon themselves for survival dominates a herd's behavior. They aren't like cattle; goats can't be pastured all summer and easily driven back to the barn in the autumn.

It is just the opposite for short periods of time. Cows that have been milked and have had their fill of hay and grain won't come back when called. They must be fetched. But a shepherd can call a herd of hungry goats from their browsing. Boys of nine and younger have controlled huge herds for centuries in Europe and Asia because goats can be managed easily. A handler may appear to be following a herd when driving it, but if that person should turn and go back, so will the goats.

Bovine and caprine comparisons reveal other differences. Cows are introverts, shy by nature, and cautious. Goats are flamboyant and extroverted; they have playful minds and enjoy challenges. Goats are daredevil enough to try anything, but they soon lose interest if the results aren't up to their expectations. Cows, on the other hand, are methodical; they will try to get through a fence by working the same weak strand of wire or rail until they succeed. Goat handlers will tell you cows are messier than goats, and that the huge manure pile behind a cow tie-up and the modest mound by a goat barn are as different as Mount Everest is from a hummock called Pleasant Hill.

Goats snort like deer when they become alarmed. In the wild, they are all sentries. While browsing or chewing their cud, goats keep turning their heads to see if there is anything threatening them. And they sometimes summon a courage that few creatures are capable of displaying in emergencies. Never has this been more incredibly illustrated than in a Vietnam War film footage of a village massacre. A small herd of goats found themselves caught in rifle fire from no more than twenty feet away. Instead of fleeing, the goats turned in unison and faced the exploding weapons.

Czar

The herd comes running

Cindra with twins, Clover & Conrad

5:30 p.m.

Wish, Tat, and Cindra are lying by the gate while the others are standing around the water trough. 5:30 p.m. Sea smoke prowls the marsh basin at the mouth of Euchre Creek Road as the afternoon retreats under a cover of rearing clouds. A solitary egret stands motionless at the edge of a pool. The clouds are thickening at sea, and the wind is bringing the smell of rain. The goats appear scattered, as if they were no longer in need of a queen or dependent on physical proximity. But this is an illusion. The sound of a dog barking from the bed of a passing truck brings the three by the gate to their feet. They all draw closer and become a herd once more; a unit alert and ready to defend its ground. The herd moves outward from the protective center only when the sound of the barking dog grows fainter. There is a smoothing of hair when the tension is no more; a movement of twisting necks, stretched legs, and quivering tails. This signals that all is well. But Czar is left edgy. He stares beyond the enclosure. Sonny ignores his nervous pasture mate and resumes his masculine appraisal of Kiaya. She stares back with yearling fascination at the red buck's massive shoulders as he climbs the groaning wire fence.

Kiaya has entered that in-between state of having outgrown her kidhood and approaching the time of her first breeding. The age for a doe's first romantic encounter can vary from between six to twelve months, (or even later) depending on the development of the animal and the opinion of the handler. Female goats come into season every seventeen to twenty-three days, and the heat lasts from a few hours to three days. The Swiss families of goats, with their northern backgrounds, are in heat during the fall and early winter, from about mid-September through December. Pygmies and Nubians, having origins in more tropical locations, are less seasonal and may be in heat at other times of the year.

Signs of heat in doelings and adult females include loss of appetite and restlessness. But not all females show signs. The lady may act a bit strangely—nervously distracted—or slightly aggressive. Some does appear more lovesick than teenagers ill with puppy love. The suffering goat girl may moon in orbit about the swashbuckling male's fence, and if the barrier between them cannot be scaled, the doe may bleat and twitch her tail and run back and forth in the pasture.

The buck looks on nervously, obviously preoccupied and frustrated. When they finally meet there may be an initial hesitation as they circle each other and sniff. Soon, they will be drawn closer, ardently nibbling and nuzzling. Just so she doesn't take him for granted or forget his maleness, the big dude stamps at her in a stiff-legged motion. Should another buck be close by, the breeding male will interrupt his romancing long enough to bellow his rage and rush the interested bystander. Even humans are not exempt from the aggressive behavior of a mating buck. "Just don't go opening that gate now, Buddy," the male may threaten with body language. "She's staying with me!"

Czar is left edgy

Tyrel

Gretchen

6:30 p.m.

6:30 p.m. This is a secret time for the herd. Humans now are too preoccupied with the close of their working day and the beginning of leisure hours to think of goats. The evening traffic increases along Route 101 while suppers are simmering on stoves. The Toggenburgs and Nubians are getting impatient as they wait by the gate. They are wondering if Diane soon will fill their racks with hay.

The mistress of Dubl Squeez has checked on the herd again— her fourth time for the day—and after dinner and dishes she will return for the evening chores. Like so many dedicated handlers, she knows that the way of achieving a good understanding with her animals is by being aware of little things: the freshness of the water in the trough, the crispness of a good quality hay, a variety in the browsing area, and impartiality in doling out treats. Veterinarians often comment on the attitude of their goat clients. "They remind me of dog and cat lovers," said one practitioner. "They'll do anything for them."

Goats are fortunate when they have people like Diane Dishner caring for them. Without such devoted handlers, the dairy goat would be in danger of living only a marginal barnyard existence. Horses, cows, even sheep, seldom are looked upon with derision or as objects of ribaldry. There has been an unpredictability throughout mankind's association with the goat.

Celtic healers used different parts of a slaughtered goat to drive away snakes, to cure loss of sight and hearing, and to treat stomach disorders and dizziness. Bone ash from the goat was used as a tooth powder. But this animal sometimes was given a more benign regard—early man had a gentle, loving, and imaginative side— though this sensitivity didn't guarantee that the poor goat would be set free with its head and hide intact.

The earliest symbols identified the goat with peace and prosperity, and it played a prominent role in mythology. Both Zeus, the great god of the Greeks, and Dionysus, god of wine, were raised on goat's milk. Amalthea supplied milk for Zeus, and this divine doe was rewarded by being transformed into the star Capella. Her hide became the magic breastplate that protected both Zeus and Athena. Amalthea's horn became the Cornucopia, symbol of plenty. Every year the Greeks honored Dionysus with a parade, and the crowd that joined the celebration would put on goat skins and imitate caprine sounds. The Greek word for goat is "tragos" and the word for singer is "oidos." Such an imitator was called "tragos-oidos" or a goat singer—a name which developed into the modern word "tragedy." One of the twelve figures of the Zodiac was Capricorn, a goat that controlled the winter solstice. The goat also had a heavenly responsibility in Norse mythology. The chariot of Thor, Norse god of thunder, weather, and crops was pulled by goats that gave mead instead of milk. Polaris, the north star, led this mead-milking team.

From the mingling of paganism and biblical history the goat also emerges as the central demon figure. One of the better known paintings in Madrid's Prado is Francisco Goya's Sabbath, or the Gathering of Sorcerers. The he-goat monster dominates the center of the canvas, his horns entwined with leaves, and an old witch is offering him the sacrifice of a child.

A few minutes with *The American Thesaurus of Slang* reveal that prejudice is still flourishing. The word goat is used to mean a laughingstock, a junior officer in the military, a sheepherder, an inferior horse, a person being initiated into a society or order, a train's switch engine, a bucking bronco, and a drunk. Cirrus storm clouds sometimes are called goat's hair, though the light, fluffy cumulus variety of fair-weather clouds would better describe such hairs; and an old automobile is referred to as a goat's nest. There are several other definitions of disparagement just waiting for the person who enjoys downgrading this animal, for example: the goat is a sheep with a goatee or a tin can guzzler.

"I sure got your goat!" one person may say to another who has become upset over a slight or a remark. But why involve this particular creature? It never interferes with the squabbles of man. A mother once commented when seeing her daughter's herd of Nubians for the first time: "For this we sent you to college!" Back to the thesaurus, here are two more definitions under goat: a licentious or lustful man, and a West Point cadet with the lowest academic rank in his class. Finally a day doesn't go by when the overworked caprine slang expression "no kidding" isn't heard.

The kids Tyrel, Conrad and Clover

7:15 p.m.

Raindrops on the roof scamper into a downpour. 7:15 p.m. The herd is lying and standing around in the goat barn away from the storm. The first puddles appear in the yard, and these soon broaden into a miniature bay with islands and peninsulas of mud. Night begins when the daytime shadows come up missing, but in an Oregon rain the transition from daylight to darkness is instantaneous. Wish and Tracy stand in the doorway and stare at the hard-to-see shape that moments before was a flooded water trough. By the expression around their eyes and the slant of their ears, these two appear in a bad mood. That playfulness they showed earlier when they romped with the Smith girls is gone. An imaginative bystander at the doorway might think the two were gossiping as their mouths open and close. If their ruminant language could be translated, the conversation would be far from lighthearted.

"The hay will be late," says the queen, "and it rains forever."

"What a day!" sighs Tracy, quickening her cud. "I've had those two kids of mine at me since morning, and now I'm going to get wet."

"Having humans around isn't easy on a queen," declares Wish, "and that whiny camera pointing in every direction gets on my nerves."

"Being a shy Toggenburg myself, I can understand that so well," Tracy chews back. "But it's where the camera points that counts."

"Don't talk in riddles."

"I must say, for a top doe, you can be dense."

"Get huffy with me, Number Two, and I'll smash your butt!"

"All I'm trying to say is how badly we goats are photographed for shows and dairy publications. Cameras are always snapping pictures of our behinds. The only good mug shots these days are close-ups of kids advertising disbudding irons or grain pellets."

"I can't dispute that," replies the queen. "I've heard those show people describing our so-called good points as milking goats."

"You mean like 'she is long-bodied and dairy, with a level topline and rump, and a high, tightly-attached pocket-free udder with an extremely wide rear attachment.'"

"Exactly!"

Our bystander smiles but looks puzzled. Did he really make all this up? He has heard of the intelligence and sensitivity of goats, and that these four-footers have been astonishing keepers for centuries.

One handler was having difficulty receiving telephone calls in his home. The extension in the barn was the problem. For some reason the receiver kept coming off the hook. After missing several important messages, the farmer had a friend ring his number, and while the call was being placed the man rushed to the barn. He was just in time to see one of his yearling does lift the receiver from the hook with her teeth. She had taken a dislike to the noisy mechanism and knew exactly what must be done to discourage callers.

But another handler had one of his Nubian does reacting favorably to human technology. After finishing his chores at night, the man would switch off the power in the goat barn and walk back up the path to his house. "Have you left that light burning again?" his wife would ask in the morning. "I must be getting balmy," the keeper would reply. "I was sure I turned it off." This went on for several nights and the man was growing increasingly concerned about his forgetfulness. "Heaven help me!" he muttered one evening when the chores were done and he was trudging back to the house with a pail of milk. "Now I've gone and left my new jacket on one of the stalls." Afraid that the coat would be nibbled at before morning, the handler returned. The moment he opened the barn door, the power went on, and he saw the Nubian with her nose at the switch. The keeper stopped worrying about himself immediately, and the next morning when the light was found burning again, he rewired the switch to the other side of the partition.

The ideal climate for goats is created by a caring handler who keeps the atmosphere of the dairy tranquil with regularity. Goats don't like surprises and they hold fast to their habits. Spanky, a Toggenburg, was rewarded with an orange soda after winning her first grand championship at a show. From that day on, after competing, she had to be given the same treat. Spanky would brace herself like a mule and would refuse to return to her pen until the drink was produced.

Kids often forget their dams and adult does and bucks their pasture mates when separated for long periods of time. But these animals do display astonishing capabilities in recalling things they enjoy. One former keeper of two kids visited a friend who had taken over the pair. The kids were two months old and didn't recognize their former mistress—not until the woman began singing a lullaby she had sung to them frequently when they were small.

Sing to goats! What next will these keepers do to keep their caprine friends content? The possibilities are endless since goat handlers are people who must be on call at all hours and around at chore time. Looking after goats is a life-style. It would be difficult to find a more dedicated group caring for animals. The mistress of Dubl Squeez was asked: Why do you keep them? "Because I have the need to be needed," she replied, "and I like their company. They follow me about, and I am so many things to them—I like all the roles I play to make them happy."

Tracy and twins

Day's End

The day is over and the herd waits in the barn for Diane. Outside, the long slant of coastal rain obliterates the peninsulas and islands of mud in the yard. Guttural threats of a flood are roaring down drainpipes and through culverts. Beyond the goat fence, a loose sheet of corrugated roofing on the wood products mill thunders back at the sky. The landscape has become a shapeless obsidian. This is no night for visitors or bystanders.

The goats rest on the morning hay they scattered in their rush to be first. If the evening had been warm and dry, they would have stayed by the gate and watched for the lights of the vehicle approaching the driveway. Now, they lie separate in the dark, each in hairy suspension, while they think of the full racks and a cushiony layer of bedding to replace the slightly damp floor covering under them.

Their anticipation of the evening meal is intense. It takes more than the morning rush at the hayracks, the sharing of treats, grain, and a day of browsing between naps and ruminant tranquil spells to satisfy their appetites. It would be unthinkable to have the routine of being fed and bedded delayed much longer. They know that soon the sound of an engine will join the storm's chorus and every light in the barn will be on.

For a moment, the rain abates. Cindra goes to the doorway and looks out in the direction of the water trough. There is only a velveteen twill of darkness and mist. The twins have nursed her into a thirst more powerful than her dread of getting wet. She detonates from the barn with neck twisting and udder swaying. Within inches of the trough, she stiffens into a full stop and noses her way to the hidden tank. The coolness of the water is slightly tainted with saline from the long Oregon beaches and the stampeding clouds above a shifting sea. Cindra nuzzles the rippled surface before nibbling a taste. Then she draws the dampness into her mouth and down the long straight lining of her throat in rhythmic gulps. Another sweep of rain tatters the nearby hillsides. Cindra explodes into another splashing gallop. Once inside the barn, she shakes free her coat of raindrops as Tracy butts Cindra's backside for Nubian carelessness.

In the ebony cave of a corner, the kids lie hidden. There is no danger of being trampled here as the does mill about impatiently. Only Tatiana wanders near to sniff Tania before turning back and collapsing on a sticky nest of bedding. Outside, an army of rain-drops is still goose-stepping, but the wind no longer lurches with a cruel cadence. It blunders forward slowly into the inland trees. Inside the drum of the barn, only the storm can be heard. The smaller, shriller sounds vanish in the steady uproar. Then unex-pectedly, all the light come on.

Instantly, the does are competing with the din outside. Their disharmonious bleats become louder as excitement mounts. They crowd the stock panel partition next to the milk room. Diane appears briefly before checking on the lambs in the sheep barn. Then she is back to fetch Hansel and Gretchen for the night away from their dam. The two kids are scooped up and carried out. Tracy is too eager for hay to register concern. She pushes Fawn and Giselle aside and noses the mesh of the partition.

It takes the mistress of Dubl Squeez about an hour to attend to everyone in the evening—about the same time as the morning chores. Diane hurries from shed to shed, again caught in her routine. There are lambs to look after, rabbits to feed, a scattering of grain for the bantams, and ample bedding in the sheep and goat barns. The herd is excited when the hay is brought in to fill the racks.

This is a time when the intricate order of dominance is tested thoroughly. Squabbles break out, and the ritualistic dance of shoving and butting begins. This is my place and mine alone—Tracy's body language suggests as she shoulders Tatiana aside. I am higher up than you, you long-posted Nubian, says Tatiana, as she in turn maneuvers Cindra away from a rack. Then Fawn and Giselle collide in a smashing headlock that settles nothing. Only Wish is privileged to decide where she wants to feed, and this is done without controversy. Soon, they settle down, after pulling wasteful clumps in their rush.

On the other side of the driveway, in a shelter that was once a small house, Sonny and Czar are bedded for the night. The Toggenburg buck hesitates a moment, giving Sonny the first dive into the hay. It would be unthinkable for Czar to challenge this Nubian that is so sure of himself.

Suddenly, as it so often happens in an Oregon downpour, a quick clearing of clouds reveals a well-nailed sky of stars. The wind slackens as the eye of the storm passes overhead. Only the trees wringing their leaves keep alive the sound of rain.

Diane finishes her chores, turns out the lights, and double-checks the gate. As she backs out of the driveway, her headlights shine on Sonny and Czar. Their eyes are jeweled by the glare as they turn to watch her leave.

The goats are eating their hay slowly now. They are nearly full and satisfied. Tatiana and Cindra check on their twins asleep in the corner of the goat barn before wandering out to the trough for water. Wish backs away from the rack and selects her place to sleep for the night. Tracy, too, has had enough and is ready now for her cud. Fawn settles close to Tracy—glad that the twins are gone. Giselle is next to Wish. Tat and Cindra find places near their young. The yearling, Kiaya, tramples a nest of bedding near Cindra.

In the doorway, there is the sound of ruffled feathers and the silhouette of a damp bantam hen stretching her wings. She struts forward in the dark, and without hesitation she roosts on Tatiana's back. For the past two nights she has slept in the goat barn—twice on Cindra and now Tat. One by one, the does fall asleep over their cud. Only Cindra stares into the night, her mouth slowing as her eyelids get heavier. She sighs and shifts her weight away from her heavy udder. Then they are all asleep.